# minedition

North American edition published 2020 by minedition, New York

Text copyright © 2012 Sueli Menezes
Illustrations copyright © 2012 Annika Siems
Coproduction with Michael Neugebauer Publishing Ltd., Hong Kong.
Rights arranged with "minedition ag", Zurich, Switzerland. All rights reserved.

Michael Neugebauer Publishing Ltd.,
19 West 21st Street, #1201, New York, NY 10010
e-mail: info@minedition.com
This book was printed in May 2020 at Hong Kong Discovery Printing Company Limited.
3/F., Blue Box Factory Building, 25 Hing Wo Street, Tin Wan, Aberdeen, Hong Kong, China
Typesetting in Goudy Old Style
Library of Congress Cataloging-in-Publication Data available upon request.

ISBN 978-1-6626-5003-1
10 9 8 7 6 5 4 3 2 1
First Impression

For more information
please visit our website:
www.minedition.com

# One Boy's Choice

Written by Sueli Menezes

Translated by Kathryn Bishop

Illustrated by Annika Siems

"We will catch a big fish, and I'll pull it out of the water all by myself!
I'll show you," said the little boy to his friends. He was so excited because
tomorrow he would go fishing with his grandad. But his friends weren't
interested; they just laughed at the little boy, as usual.

Very early the next morning, the boy and his grandad set out in their canoe. The boy was thrilled to spend the whole day fishing with his grandad. For as long as he could remember, his grandad had told him stories about the different fish that lived in the great river.

Grandad sat in front while the boy
sat at the other end of the canoe.
Smoothly they paddled the wooden
boat through the deep jungle.
Today was the day.
He would show the other boys;
he would bring home a big fish.

As grandad steered them through
The great water-lilies,
the boy said,
"Grandad, tell me the story
about the fish that live under
the water-lilies, please!"

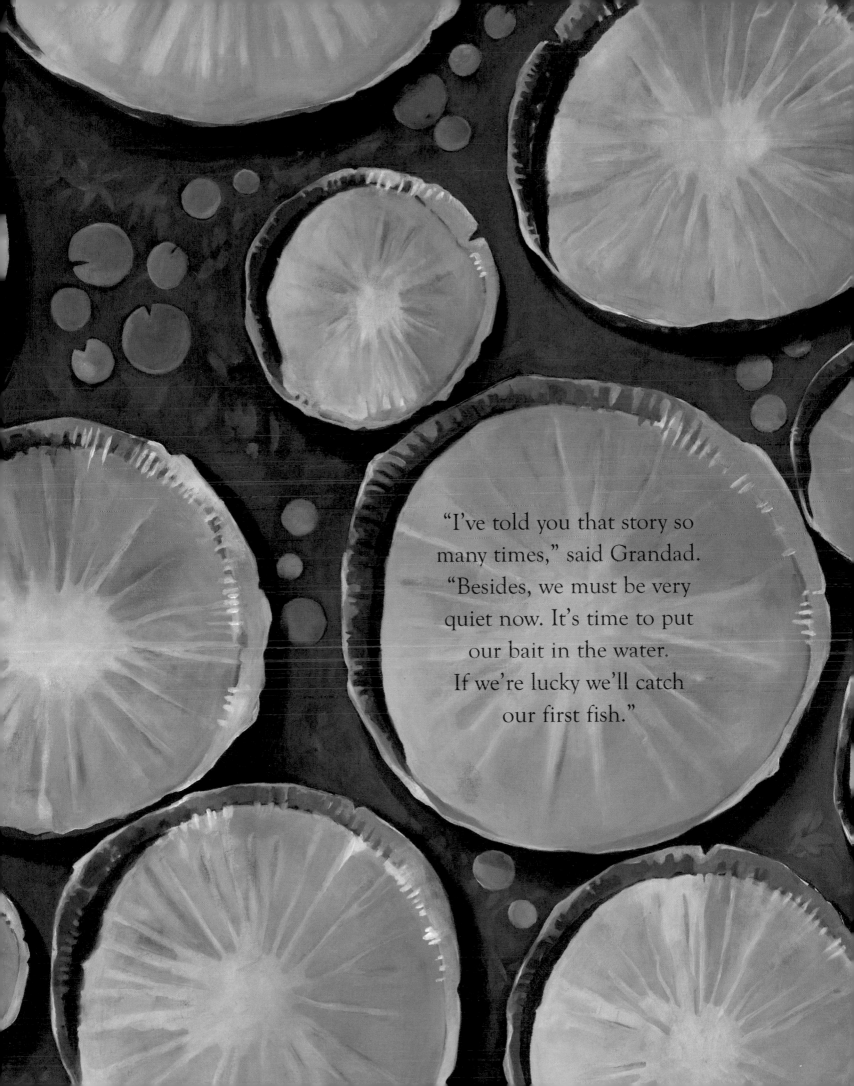

"I've told you that story so
many times," said Grandad.
"Besides, we must be very
quiet now. It's time to put
our bait in the water.
If we're lucky we'll catch
our first fish."

The little boy watched the water intently.
He dreamed of coming home with a really big fish.

They waited patiently for the first bite.
They waited and waited, and waited
some more.
Nothing!

They paddled a little further and tried
another spot, but still they had no luck.
It was as if the river had hidden all its fish!
"Don't be sad," Grandad said to the little boy.
"We'll cast the net instead. Then you'll see
how many big fish we can catch."

"Okay, Grandad," said the boy as helped
him toss the net into the water.
The net had a little piece of wood attached
that floated on the top of the water; when
it started to move back and forth, that
would mean a fish had swum into their net.

Grandad and the boy watched and waited.
They could see the whole river.
Mesmerized, the boy kept staring at the
floating wood while Grandad told stories
about the different fish that lived under
the water-lilies.

Hours passed with hardly
a motion, when suddenly,
several little fish leapt out of
the water before disappearing again.
"Grandad," asked the boy, "why do the
fish jump out of the water like that?"

"Perhaps they're trying to tell us something important," said Grandad quietly.
"Come, let us check the net; perhaps we have been lucky."

"Oh, Grandad, look at the big fish!" shouted the boy.
"It's a water-lily fish!" He had never seen an Arowana,
but he had heard Grandad's stories about them.

"No, I'm afraid this one is not for us," said Grandad.
"We must set him free so he can swim away."

"But Grandad, he's the biggest fish in the net. We have to take this one.
You know how important it is for me to bring home a great fish!"

"Come, help me free the fish, and I'll explain to you
why we must set him free."

Gently, Grandfather took the fish out of the net. "You see the little fish in his mouth?" he said. "They are his children. The male Arowana are the best dads in the world. For a month, the tiny fish live in their father's mouth, where he keeps them safe. During this time, no one should catch the Arowana because his children would die, too. The Arowana are important to us because they eat the mosquitoes that make people ill."

Grandad put the fish in the boy's hands and said, "You must decide what is more important–taking the fish to show your friends, or letting this dad and his children live peacefully in the great river."

With a little smile, the boy carefully
put the fish and his children back
into the water.
The old man hugged his grandson.

"I am so very proud of you," he said.
"Today you have become a really
grown-up boy."